The Bag

by Diana Noonan
illustrated by Pat Reynolds

Harcourt

SCHOOL PUBLISHERS

Printed in the United States of America

ISBN 10: 0-15-351218-0
ISBN 13: 978-0-15-351218-6

Ordering Options
ISBN 10: 0-15-351211-3 (Grade 1 Advanced Collection)
ISBN 13: 978-0-15-351211-7 (Grade 1 Advanced Collection)
ISBN 10: 0-15-358015-1 (package of 5)
ISBN 13: 978-0-15-358015-4

2 3 4 5 6 7 8 9 10   179   15 14 13 12 11 10 09 08 07

Pam has a cap.

Pam has a little cat.

Pam has a pink pillow,
too.

Can the pillow go in
the bag?

No. The bag is too little.

Dad has come to help
Pam.

Now the pillow can go in
the bag.